DEDICATIONS

I dedicate this book to my two sons Quentin and
Xavier Brown who are excellent and original in every way. To
my hometown of Hollydale in Ohio where I learned you can
make mistakes and still come home.

- T. B.

Dedicated to anyone who has ever made a friend
out of an enemy.

- S. B.

TABLE OF CONTENTS

List of Full Page Illustrations

Map of Hollydale, Springfield Township

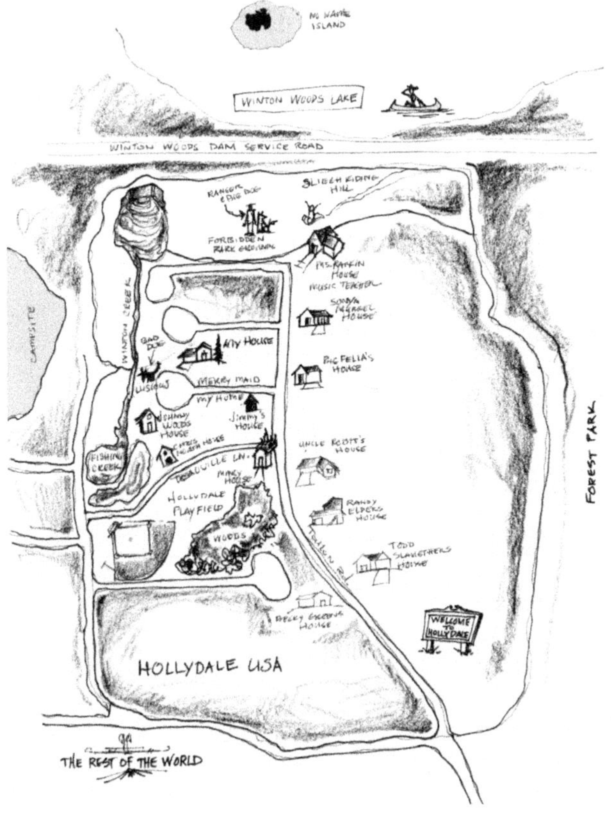

PoP
BIG
STINGER

STORY ONE

THE BUS BULLY MYSTERY

Told By little Manny McDowell

Natty was one of the three bully sisters. These sisters were bad, like a swarm of bees. They constantly teased and ridiculed kids. Natty was the oldest, with a brow like Frankenstein. Kat was the middle sister. They called her Kat because she could scratch you to the bone with her claw-like nails. The youngest was Shane. She was the worst—a bona fide spitter and had a mouth like a seasoned sailor.

Each school day, the bus ride began with these three brutal chicks. They would get on the bus, turn to find a seat, and Scan the crowd as if all the kids were prime, fresh meat. They even put the bus driver's stomach in knots, Making him drive by kids waiting at the bus stops. He'd pull up to a corner full of kids and big sister Natty would cut her eyes and snarl, "Did I tell you to stop?"

These sisters ruled the bus like it was their personal bully domain. They ruled with pain and pure shame. This day, Manny sat quietly at the back of the bus, Apart from the rest, drawing. Little sister Shane walked over to take a look And spit right inside Manny's sketchbook. "Only sissies draw, haven't you learned?"
The bus got so quiet, you could hear a screw turn. Manny's eyes welled with tears and his throat got dry. All he felt was rage as a tear fell from his eye. The kids stood and watched. What would Manny do?

As the bus stopped at the school, the windows were all in a haze. Manny calmly stated, "This is the last time you terrorize us." What happened next is the stuff of legend, to this day. So legendary, not one kid would say.

When the kids piled out, they were bursting with glee, Something had happened that no one could foresee. The kids weren't tortured, they had a spring in their step, No fear, no shakes, each happier than the next.

When Manny walked off the bus, he was calmer than any. His sketchbook neatly tucked under his arm. The three sisters emerged in peace, to everyone's alarm. The crowd of kids parted so they could make their way. Something had happened to the bully sisters that day.

Manny did something, no doubt Because those sisters were changed. These chicks had suddenly turned meek, Free of the filthy cracks and absent from of all that fuss. Changed by an incident at the back of the bus.

Some say the truth is locked in the pages of Manny's sketchbook, A place we may never have the chance to look. One thing is for sure, Manny tamed that beastly crew, So much so they finally have nice things to look forward to. When asked what happened, not one kid will say.

Not a word about what they witnessed that day.

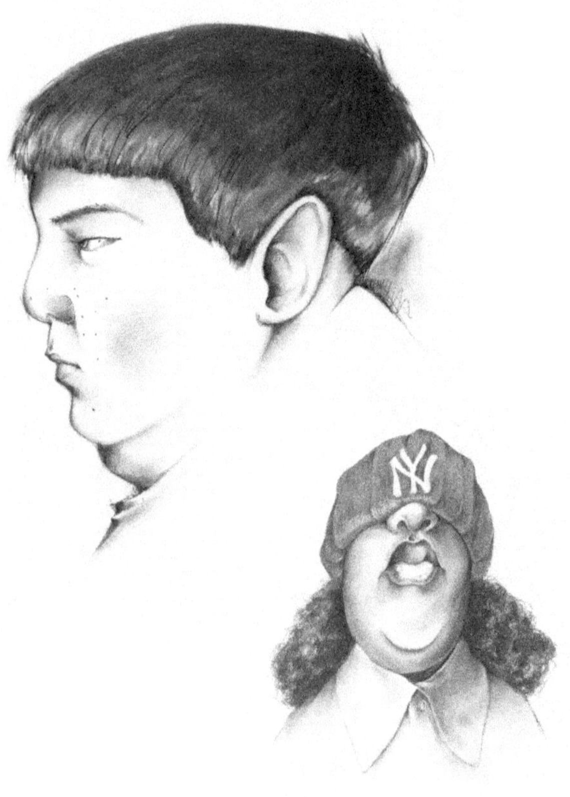

STORY TWO

THE BULLY BROWN DAYS
Told by Bully Brown

Bully Brown was the meanest kid around.
Part of his fame was his bully gang.

These dudes were evil, that's a fact.
They shouted, teased, and simply had no tact.

There was big Robby Tom, on the football team.
There was Stinky E, who never smelled clean.

A kid named Rashawn, who they called Baby Ray,
He always had something nasty to say.

Last, but not least, was a tall kid named Sneak,
Who never smiled because he had no teeth.

But the scariest of the crowd was Bully Brown,
Not only loud, he had his own evil cloud.
I'd seen him do the worst things,
I'd seen him step on other kids' dreams.

But one day … the last straw … that was it.
Little Manny McDowell wasn't taking another fat lip.

Bully Brown took Manny's lunch,
Ate his candy bar, and left him with a punch.

The next day after gym would be the day,
Manny McDowell would finally have his say.

Kids knew the story, the rumor spread like lice.
No one counted on Manny to win this fight.

When Manny arrived, fear was in the air.
A crowd of kids gathered to see if he would dare.

Manny clinched his fists, gave Bully Brown a stare,
He tightened his lip, threw a fit, and shouted,
"I AIN'T GOIN NOWHERE!"

Manny slammed his sketchbook on the ground.
As the book flew open, no one made a sound.

When the pages settled, everyone looked down.
A drawing with bold words read:
BULLY BROWN IS A CLOWN.

The crowd roared with laughter. Kids held their stom-
achs in pain,
While Bully Brown sank his head in total shame.

Even his gang laughed at what the drawing said.
Soon the evil cloud began to leave Bully Brown's head.

The room was quiet as Bully Brown's
eyes began to thaw.
He walked right up to Manny and said, "I didn't know
you could draw."

From that day on, Bully Brown and Manny were cool.
Somewhere, deep down inside, Bully Brown realized he
had been a fool.

Bully Brown and Manny became good friends.
All because one fateful day, when a drawing brought
terror to an end.

Manny still draws nearly every day or whenever he has
the time.
I will always remember what happened when one kid
decided to draw the line.

9
No
Sissy Locker
Mc Mike

STORY THREE

LOCKER ROOM SWEETS

The eighth-grade boys' locker room was usually a place wrought with the unimaginably dense smell of funky feet laced with I-forgot-my-deodorant. This day was slightly different as I detected the faintest trace of chocolate. Caramel and peanut smells got louder as I passed his locker. Church boy was at it again. Just my luck. Everyone was in such a rush to get on the playfield, he had neglected to fully close his locker. I loved the candy bars he sold. A solid block of chocolate unlike the standard off-the-shelf, pocket-sized versions—the kind that stuck out of your pocket like a tasty trophy teasing those who dreamed of getting a bite. The kind you could only eat a little at a time or you would get the equivalent of brain freeze but only from chocolate. You stupid kid. Why would you tempt me like this, when you know I can't resist? I'm as weak as a diabetic kid in the parking lot of a fast-food joint. I'd seen church boy peddle his wares like a pro; so good, so smooth, like a chocolate game show host and we were just waiting to see who he'd choose to be his next con-testant. He didn't discriminate. First were the cutest girls that ran up to him, like he was their lost, lonely boyfriend. They surrounded him, rolling his name off their lips like a sweet, soft apology; as though they wanted his forgiveness for the long absence. Even the coolest guys showed him a sample of what ac-ceptance was like amongst the elite at the sound of those six sweet words: "I have candy bars for sale." The nerds bought five bars at a time, like the candy bars were sweet, intellectual-boosting substances from only which they could unlock its secrets. Then, there were the teachers. He could soften the crabbiest, meanest, stiffest, and sulkiest of the bunch. They acknowledged him like he was the saint of Princeton Junior High.

Five times I tried to barter, bargain, and trade with this guy for his precious church candy bars. Not a chance. He was tighter than a woodshop table-vice. I begged him, even misquoted some Scriptures as an attempt to show some empathy. Nothing worked. The only thing more devout to him than church were his precious candy bars. Who sells candy bars for a church anyway? Some dim whit who thinks he's earning points to help get into heaven. Please. I think he really believes Jesus cares about his candy bars, as if He was keeping track of how many he sold. You should have given me one, church boy. At least on loan or something. What makes you the holy saint of chocolate bars sanctioning? Who said you can pick and choose who gets a taste of your precious bars? Well, this day I think Jesus is turning his cheek. I think this is a mere reverse blessing in disguise, tailormade for me. Otherwise, if Jesus didn't want me to have them, why would he let you leave without locking your locker this time? Yeah, I think it's a sign.

As I eased open the locker, I discovered it was even better than I thought. Three luscious candy bars were sitting in a box, neatly tucked beside an envelope. I hurriedly slipped them out, a caramel, a solid chocolate, and a krispy chocolate bar. While I slowly eased the last bar out of the box, it fell at an angle, hitting the inside of the locker hard enough to flip the envelope full of money onto the locker room floor. All I could think was that for some reason God was blessing me more than I ever thought I deserved. Twenty-three bucks and three candy bars—

this was sweet.

I was juiced as I walked out of the locker room and into the hallway leading to the door that would take me to the playfield. As I looked up, anticipating the activity on the field I was missing, I saw him rushing toward me. Church boy, at full speed, ran down the hallway and past the water fountain. I stopped and stared at him while thinking, Jesus, is this a joke you are playing on me or something? I paused, expecting him to confront me about his precious candy bars. Nothing. Instead, as he ran past me into the locker room, he said, "We just chose flag football teams, man. I think the Red team has you." I rubbed my stomach as though I had just eaten a five-course meal and headed to the field toward the red team as they were passing out flags. Everyone was looking at me, really just staring at me, like they could see through me or something. No one said a word, just stared. A few guys smirked and grinned as I faintly heard some commotion over my right shoulder. I finally reached the guys on the red team. "What's up? Can we do this?" I said with supreme confidence. They laughed. "What's up? Why ya'll laughin' at me, man?"

"I think you have a problem, dude., Look," one of them said.

As I turned around, I saw a teammate struggling to hold on to church boy. Church boy was crying and wailing, arms flinging, feet kicking. Big Robert was trying to hold him and calm him down at the same time, but not having much success. Robert outweighed church boy by at least 110 pounds. As another kid walked over to help hold church boy, church boy pointed and screamed at me, "I gonna get you! I'm gonna get you! I'm gonna get you!" His eyes were red as blood and tears streamed down his face and his teeth clinched like a mad boar. He was a foot away from me when the gym teacher lunged his large, muscular arm between us. Incident avoided so I thought.

As I walked to art class next day, a bunch of classmates stood in the doorway of the classroom. I could hear their laughter as I approached. Church boy was already sitting down at his easel, fully immersed into his drawing. Art was his favorite subject; the guy could draw anything. He never talked when he was in art class, even if you wanted a candy bar. This was more than religion to him, more than selling candy bars or even the attention it brought him. He was an art nerd of the highest order, and it was the week we had to turn in our submissions for the monster poster contest. Church boy came in second place last year, which no seventh grader had ever done. The rest of us just watched as the great artists in the school competed, like polished, elite athletes in their sports; leaving us mere mortals gazing with disbelief at their unworldly magic with a pencil. Today was the day they would hang the finalists in the main hallway for all the school to see. Seventh and eighth graders competing for the top prize of the whole school.

A massive group of kids crowded around, laughing and admiring, pointing at their favorite posters. As I approached, the crowd seemed to quiet to a hush and part, leaving a trail to church boy's poster. As I looked up, I was still wondering why everyone was so quiet when I stepped up. It hit me like I had been punched in the gut by a three-hundred-pound boxer. I had absolutely no defense at all, no sizable response that even came close to mounting a formidable response; just a blank gaze at what I would have to live down the rest of the

school year for sure, maybe longer. There I was, im-
mortalized in the poster, just the two of us, full center
composition. We were clad superhero style, muscles
and all, like an epic comic book cover that had just
been released. He had drawn chocolate around my
mouth, while my left hand was holding an unwrapped
candy bar. A piece a chocolate was flying out of my
mouth from the force of a punch delivered to my jaw
by none other than church boy. I endured a relentless
onslaught of laughter and grins in the halls for what
seemed a lifetime after that day. I wished he had just
punched me when we were on the field, in the flesh.
This was triple worse, quadruple worse. We didn't
even fight but somehow I had gotten beat up bad.
The kind of beating that people would cheer about
even if I sought revenge. I couldn't fight this fight.
As embarrassing as it was, the only thing I could do
was bear it and somehow hope the pain from this

nonphysical confrontation faded.

I'd been in fights before, and was on the winning end of most. That's what bullies do, we win fights all the time. But this was different. I was beaten before the first punch was thrown—and hurting long after. That dude kicked my butt with a beating that lasted my entire middle school life. So many times I wanted to go up to him and just smash him right there in the hall. So many times I wanted to call him out in front of everybody and end this thing once and for all. But he kept right on selling his beloved candy bars just as if nothing ever happened between us. In fact, church boy was more popular than ever after that. He won second place again in the monster contest. I always knew the kid could draw, I just never suspected he would manage to teach me a lesson by merely lifting a pencil.

STORY FOUR

Don't Come Home

Some guys were cousins for real. Some were cousins because they were best friends. And others were cousins just because they were tired of getting beat up. I had a friend like the latter of those examples. I didn't find that out, though, until it was too late. I played in Jay's garage almost every day after school, me and the guys. This particular day, just a few of us were hanging around until Ceedog decided to hang out with us. Not good, because Ceedog was the towering neighborhood bully. The kind you just avoided because you never knew what mood he was in. Fortunately, Jay and I were able to avoid his abuse because we both had attractive sisters Ceedog wanted to impress and nothing killed your chances better than beating up a cute girl's little brother. The other guys weren't that fortunate, to say the least; so they slowly, one-by-one, went home. So it was down to Ceedog, Jay, and I hanging out in Jay's garage, lifting weights and playing music.

Now Ceedog lived on the next street to ours and had a couple of sisters and brothers, most of which were older than us. I think his dad had left his mom years ago and everybody in the neighborhood knew the kids were out of control. Jay had been in Ceedog's house once and said it was like visiting a supersized roach motel. He said the roaches practically told you that you needed permission to open the refrigerator. He said he saw roaches so big they were trying on clothes in one of the rooms. Ceedog's house was so bad the garbagemen hated stopping there on trash day. The last guy that stopped to pick up the trash got into a fistfight with a couple of rats right there, in front of the house. His partner had to jump

out of the truck to help him.

Ceedog was one of those tragic guys who seemed to be trapped in his own sad circumstances in life. His clothes were rarely clean, and he always bullied kids for lunch money because he never had any. I never had trouble with him because I always packed my lunch. Ceedog was nasty and mean, with no sight of better days in his future from what we could see.

We didn't know how this day would end and

chose to live under our false sense of security a little longer. Good music was playing, the weight-lifting was going well—until Jay's sister came in to tell us to turn the music down a little. This got Ceedog into a love gaze. He turned and asked Jay to hook him up with his sister. Jay responded that she had a boy-friend and that was not going to happen. Cee didn't care about a boyfriend. He would find the kid, punch his lights out, and force him to break up with her if he wanted. Cee simply didn't care. "Hook me up, Jay," said Ceedog.

"Man, I told you, she has a boyfriend. She in love with that dude," replied Jay.

"That dude has a car too. You can't compete with that dude," I said boldly. Cee turned to me with a scowl—and I knew I was in a little trouble. "Who asked you, punk?" Ceedog replied. I wondered how I should respond. I knew a bad response could take Ceedog to crazy bullyland, and I would end up get-ting a beat down and then spend day after day explaining to everyone what happened, or I could sink like a rock and hide in my self-made bully shame hole and cower like I usually did. Like an alarm, a voice in my head shouted: "Not this time!" I paused, waited for a moment while I finished putting down the weight, and calmly said, "Dude, you know I'm right. You don't have a chance."

Well, Cee was insulted more than I expected. I thought he would recognize that I was trying to help him not get embarrassed, but he didn't take it that way; in fact, he took it a whole different way that evolved into a Neanderthal's nightmare. Things got tense quickly—and surprisingly, Jay actually sided with the Cee. So there I was, alone. Ceedog stood over me like a puffed-up bear before a meal and Jay was in the background instigating him on. Cee threatened to pound me if I said one more word.

I did. He shoved me so hard I fell against the garage wall, knocking down half of the tools. I hastily darted out of the garage, down the driveway, and headed to my house across the street with tears in my eyes. I could hear Jay calling me a cry baby in the background. As I retreated to the comfort of my own front yard, where I would surely be safe, I thought to myself how quickly things had turned bad and how my friend had changed like a chameleon, from bully survivor to full-blown bully instigator. But that was the least of my problems. I was about to face a whole new issue that I definitely was not prepared for. Mama. I looked up at the front door, with thoughts of safety fresh in my grasp, only to find my mother standing on the porch with an all too familiar stance. One hand on the hip and a look of disgust only a mother can project. I was about to explain to her what had happened when she spit out four words that struck fear and anger in me. "Get back over there!" she shouted. "And don't come back until you get him!" mama demanded.

I felt something I had never felt before: a mix of anger, fear, and newfound courage. I abruptly turned and stomped toward the street. By the time I got to the street, that stomp had turned into a rage-filled run. When I looked up, I saw fear creep into the eyes of Ceedog and Jay. Before I could get to them, though, they both turned and ran toward Jay's house. I ran after them, completely out of my mind with anger. I was screaming at the top of my lungs, "I'm going to beat the skin off you, Cee!" I remember letting out a tribal, warlike sound which I think even scared my mom! They barely made it through the front door and locked it before I reached it.

I didn't get to skin them, but maybe this was better. As I walked back home, I looked up at my mom and saw something in her face that I had not seen before. She had a self-assured look that seemed to say that, finally, she knew I would be okay. Like she could finally settle inside herself knowing that little Manny was going to be okay. She slowly turned and walked into the house with a confidence that made me proud I had listened to her. It was as if she knew I had needed to learn to trust myself. I followed her inside, and she never spoke about the incident again. But I knew we had reached a triumph in our mother-son relationship.

Usually dads were the ones who made their kids stand up to bullies and moms wanted you to talk it out. Not my mom, though. She had other plans for me which did not include talking things out. She wanted me to learn to stand up for myself when no one else would; when no one else was around. She knew I needed to learn to trust myself more—and she knew how to make that happen.

I always wanted Mom to be proud of me. And I could tell she was as she made me a peanut butter and jelly sandwich.

31

THE
BOSS

STORY FIVE

Introducing A Girl Named Guppy Shalinqua ...That Evil So And So
Told By little Manny MacDowell

Hi, my name is Manny and I would like to introduce you to a little girl named Guppy Shalinqua. An evil girl, far worse than evil, quite hateful, I should say. I think she was born in hell and someone left the gate open. Shalinqua had always terrorized us, and I was her target on a daily basis—I was her little brother. I rarely said her name, for fear it would conjure a punch or a kick in the knee. She did not need a reason to torture you, just saying her name could set her off like a box of fireworks. I'll tell you some of her worst deeds, and I'm sure you will agree this babe was pure evil.

Over the years, I've tried many times to find out how Guppy became so evil. When she was born, our mom had to work, so Guppy stayed with our aunt. Aunt Jess was mean as ten sawed-off snakes and cursed bad enough to make angels weep, but she was the only one mama could find to watch Guppy. We always surmised this was Guppy's ruin.   Aunt Jess lived in the heart of the ghetto on the wickedest street in the town. Hustlers, gang bangers, and all sorts in between, hung out there. It was no place for a small baby, let alone any decent person trying to take care of a family. Jess lived on the corner of the main block, we called it downtown. The building was an old storefront with apartments above.

Aunt Jess's apartment was up a long flight of stairs along the side of the building that led you to the back. I shook with fright every time we had to visit Jess. The long hallway leading to her apartment was dark and dingy, and smelled like cat piss. Every few feet there would be a roach on the wall, looking at us as if we were its next meal. Jess never came to the door, she just yelled, "Come in!" when you knocked. Her place smelled like a mix between a bar and a wet basement all the time. She never cleaned, and you could see the remnants of last night's partying on her coffee table each day. I don't think she liked me at all; actually, I don't think she like kids. Period. Come to think of it, she might not have liked people altogether.

It was always dark in her apartment, and you could never quite saw her face completely. She never said much, choosing to grunt most of her responses. When she did speak, it was fast, as though she was afraid someone was listening to her and she didn't want them to hear what she was saying. Guppy would be sitting in the middle of the floor as usual, screaming at the top of her lungs. I always stood just inside the door too afraid to get anywhere close to aunt Jess. Mama always thanked Jess and said she would pay her when she had the chance. Jess just grumbled and stared through the darkness of the room. I could hear her say under her breath, "What you lookin at?" I felt as if I would piss my pants that moment. I had the feeling Guppy didn't like being there anymore than I did. The longer we stayed, the more it felt like I would suffocate from fear, but Mama would put her hand around my shoulder and say, "Come on, baby," which gave me the comfort I needed to reach the end of the corridor to the outside stairs.

I knew Guppy didn't like me from the get go. I think it was because she was the baby until I came along and messed that up. I lived with Aunt Percy, everybody's favorite aunt, until I was about three years old. Mama finally had enough money saved to get us all a place together. Everyone was happy except Guppy, she cried all the time. My role as the recipient of her angry tantrums began early in life. Anytime Mama would leave us alone, I got it, and got it bad. When we took baths together, I got it. When we ate dinner together, I got it. At playtime, I got it. Even naptime was a painful event. I got punched so much I thought it was normal.

Yeah, Guppy used me to sharpen her evil. I was practice for later and greater evil exploits. It would begin in the morning and last all day long. Guppy was like an alarm clock, but instead of a buzz or bell, it was "GET UP, STUPID!" Sometimes just a kick in the ribs would awaken me. I made the mistake of using the bathroom before her one morning. WHAM! My fingers shut up in the bathroom door. They still hurt. My fingers swelled instantly as I fell to the floor, throbbing in pain. I lay on the floor, crying for at least an hour. Guppy did not care. Her heart was as hard as a fossilized tree stump. After she finished washing her face, brushing her teeth, and combing her hair, she opened the bathroom door and stepped right over me like I was a piece of chewing gum. Just when I thought she might look back to show pity on my soul, she said, "Shut up that crying, you little sissy," and she slammed her bedroom door.

She was like a time bomb, a walking sore dripping with anger. A bag of seething rattlesnakes with the ability to punch your eyes loose at any time. This babe was no joke.

This night, though, Guppy would meet her match. Mama had taken just about enough of Guppy's angry tantrums for a day. She took Guppy in her bedroom to take care of business. It sounded like twelve cats fighting in there … then silence. Complete quiet. The storm was over. Mama came out of the bedroom with a look of supreme power on her face. She walked past me and went downstairs to prepare dinner. Guppy walked out of her bedroom and into the bathroom, tears still in her eyes from the beating. I had never seen Guppy so serene during dinner. I thought to myself, Is this the beginning of a changed Guppy, a more respectable Guppy, one whom would take orders with the grace of a nun? Guppy walked past me into the kitchen to do the dishes; tears were still in the corners of her eyes.

As she walked past me, the pain from my throbbing fingers reminded me that it would take much more than one spanking to whip this chick back into a mild-mannered little girl. Maybe it was a start though.

That night we did the dishes together. It was a good night.

STORY SIX

Sunday Evilness

We always went to church on Sunday. Always. All day. Always. Guppy simply hated going to church. She hated getting up early. She hated getting dressed up. She really hated getting her hair done. She was always the last one to get in the car in the morning, which made our stepdad furious.

I usually sat in the backseat with Guppy. I gave her space when she was this angry because it was dangerous to agitate her any more than she was already. When we arrived at church, Guppy never sat with us. I think she sat by herself to brew up things she could do to us later. She hated the music. She hated the preacher. She even hated the nice, little deacon who came around with the offering plate. She would snarl at him like a pack of wild wolves. I always kept one eye open during prayer just to check on Guppy. The only time Guppy perked up was during benediction. She was happier than a dog in a bone shop. The be-tween service meals made her ecstatic. She would skip around the restaurant, singing and eating every-thing in sight. She would terrorize the other kids at church to the brink of tears. I was glad it wasn't me, but I sure felt sorry for those kids. The longer we stayed at church, the worse Guppy became. I could always tell when she was about to explode. Pretty soon, everyone began to move away from her, even the preacher began to sweat. By now, it was too late and I just sat back to watch the show. Then it hap-pened ... BOOM.

A tantrum like you'd never believe—right in the mid-dle of church service. She was the queen of tan-trums. Building and collapsing tantrums. The kind of tantrums that needed prayer. Once again, Guppy had ruined another day for everyone. Everyone having a bad time but her, just the way she liked it. During the drive home, we sat in the backseat of the car, just as we had on the way to church. The only difference was that Guppy had a smile on her face. A frightfully evil smile; just the way she liked it.

POP
DRI

STORY SEVEN

DADDY THIEF

It was the third Saturday. 'The time of the month I enjoyed most and Guppy hated in her bones. It was the day her biological dad came to pick her up. Our mom never married Guppy's dad, so he came to pick her up once month for as long as I can remember. He was a nice man; tall, dark, and handsome. And he always drove a nice car. The only problem was, Guppy hated him and the only way she would go with him was if I went along.

Willie Lou was always late, but I didn't mind be-cause I knew I would enjoy myself. Guppy didn't talk the whole time we spent with him. She just sat in the backseat brewing. Her dad was great. He took us to nice restaurants and great movies. He even took us

to the drag races. He always taught us something.
Guppy never wanted anything, so I got everything.
Cotton candy, hot dogs, souvenirs, everything. I
never had to ask for a thing.

　　　The more I got, the madder Guppy became.
By the time we returned home, she was boiling with
anger. Guppy would burst out of the car, run straight
to the front door, and march into the kitchen where
Mama was standing. I knew I was in trouble, big
trouble. Guppy immediately began to spin a web
of deceit. She told Mama how I ate all the hot dogs
and cotton candy at the movies. How I rode in the
front seat the whole time and how I had two large
freezes at the park. How I got an expensive souvenir. "Mama, Manny ruined everything," Guppy cried.
"He begged the whole time, Mama." The room went
silent while steam passed through Guppy's nostrils.

　　　Mama calmly folded her arms, looked at
Guppy, then looked at me. My heart felt heavier
than an elephant's butt. I thought to myself, You're

going to get it kid. Just as I was prepared for my mother's full wrath, she turned to Guppy and said in a soft voice, "If you wanted something, why didn't you ask for it, Guppy?"

Guppy's face went pale, like a powdered-sugar do-nut. Her jaw dropped to her shoelaces. She glared at me with eyes that could melt Mt. Everest. "I hate you!" she screamed and tore upstairs like a mad tor-nado. She never even said goodbye to her dad. I thanked him for a great time and proudly walked up the stairs to find a place for my souvenir. I sat on my bed and thought to myself, I like third Saturdays.

STORY EIGHT

Late Again

Saturday night was my favorite time at our home. Everyone had something to do. My stepdad worked on the house, Mama watched TV, I got to finish building one of my model cars, and Guppy was going skating with Shank. Mama told Guppy the same thing every week, "Guppy, be back by ten o'clock." Guppy never listened; she always came back late, always. I think she did it just to cause trouble. Saturday night was special for me because it meant no unsuspecting backhands from Guppy, just peace and quiet.

While Mama gave Guppy her last instructions, I went to the front door to let Shank in. Shank was Guppy's best friend and lived up the street from us. When she was around Guppy, Shank became mean as a snake. "Where's Guppy, maggot boy?" Before I could answer, BOOM! right in the stomach. I limped up to my room while hearing the sounds of devilish laughter behind me.

Before I knew it, the clock flashed 9:45 pm. An unsettling feeling came over me, like the dark of summer. Guppy's going to be late again. This set off a chain of events that lasted well into Sunday morning. My stepdad would get upset when Guppy was late and storm through the house locking all the doors. Mama would try to calm him down while asking him for just a few more minutes. This meant, I had to keep watch to unlock the door when Guppy finally showed up.   My job was to stay awake until I heard Guppy coming, sneak back downstairs and unlock the door without waking our stepdad.

This night, I must have fallen asleep because when I awoke the clock was flashing 12:02 and Mama was whispering for me to go check the door. Nothing. No Guppy. Mama called Shank's house but no one answered, then she called a few of

Guppy's other friends, but no one had seen Guppy. I finally fell asleep on the living room floor and awoke with a shock to discover daylight coming through the shades. It was 8:00 am. I tiptoed into Guppy's room, wondering if I had missed her during the night. As I pushed the door open, I prayed she would be fast asleep. Empty. No Guppy anywhere. The covers were smooth as a new coat on Sunday. I knew this meant trouble.

I tried to think of all the things that could have gone wrong. Maybe Guppy got lost on the way home or, even worse, maybe she was kidnapped. Who was I fooling? If someone kidnapped Guppy, they'd pay us just to take her back. No, this was no accident. This was a Guppy Shalinqua special with all the trimmings. For all we knew, she was standing at the back door waiting for the most inopportune time to waltz into the house. Yes, this was classic Guppy.

Everyone began to prepare for church, like we did every Sunday. Still no Guppy. We all loaded into the car and I took my usual seat in the back be-hind the driver's seat. It was a little strange to look over and not see Guppy. After church, we headed straight home for Sunday afternoon dinner. Still no Guppy. I thought to myself, This is bad, very bad. Mom was unusually quiet all day.

Just as we finished dinner, I began to clear the table and heard a sound at the door. In walked Guppy, not a worried bone in her body. I stood like a statue at the kitchen sink, waiting for our stepdad and mom to explode on her. Nothing. Not a word. I thought to myself, This is strange. Guppy just stood in the middle of the kitchen, ready for a showdown. Nothing. Silence. I really got nervous. Then, in a low grumbling voice, Guppy uttered, "Aren't you go-ing to say something?"

Nothing, just silence. "Hey, aren't you mad at me for staying out all night?"

Still nothing.

By now, Guppy was turning as purple as a

beet and began to shout at the top of her lungs. "I could have been hurt! I could have been kidnapped! I could have run away or something, or even worse, got picked up hitchhiking by a murderous trucker killer!"

Just as Guppy was about to really explode with anger, Mama looked up at her and said, "I hope you had a good time, sweetie."

Guppy held her breath so long I thought she would evaporate. Then ..."Ahhhhhhhh!" Guppy let out a scream of agony.

We didn't see her the rest of the night, Wham! went her bedroom door as she locked herself in her room. Her devilish plan hadn't worked. Maybe she was losing her evil powers. Maybe Guppy wasn't in control after all.

PLEF
THE GORILLA
FIERCE GORILLA

STORY NINE

NOTHING SCARES GUPPY

Guppy wasn't afraid of anything, ever. Not monsters. Not mean dogs. Not bullies. After all, she was the king of bullies. Those mean quadruplets who lived around the corner in our neighborhood, the ones everyone was afraid of, they didn't worry Guppy. She sent them home crying. The neighborhood dog Lucius, that terrorized us when we got off the bus every afternoon, was no match for Guppy. That dog might as well have been invisible. The hoodlum boys that hung out on the corner didn't scare Guppy. When she was finished, they were crying like babies. Even the security guard at school, big Jake, the 300-pound meanie, was terrified of Guppy. Big Jake didn't scare her a bit. She tuned him out like a bad radio station.

I had never seen Guppy fear anyone or anything. I'd witnessed her getting spankings without shedding a tear. Once we took a trip to the zoo, but never saw any animals. Guppy had them shaking in their boots, afraid to come out. This babe was mean and nasty, a dreadful terror, a walking whirlpool of evil—except for one thing. In all my life, I have only found one thing that scared Guppy out of her wits.

There I was, fast asleep in the middle of the night, when a loud crash and bright lights filled my room. I loved sleeping through storms, I could dream so well. Then I felt something shivering next to me in my bed. I pulled back the covers and to my surprise, it was Guppy. Curled up like a wet puppy, shivering from head to toe. The king of Bully Mountain, the ice princess herself, the terrorizer of Terror Ville was afraid of thunder and lightning. This was the person who couldn't stand to be around me for a second; the same person who earlier had called me a "maggot boy;" the same person who punched my lights out every chance she got, for no reason at all.

57

She needed me. Guppy Lenora Shalinqua needed her little brother. I told her not to worry and drifted off to sleep. I knew tomorrow the old Guppy would be back, but for now, being needed felt just fine.

BabysittersAnonymous BA
#1 BABYSITTER
SKILLED • DEDICATED
The last call you'll ever need to make guaranteed.

STORY TEN

GUPPY BULLY SITS

This was special. I didn't have to go to church with my parents. Friday nights at church was like being in a cemetery. Most times, I was the only kid there with a bunch of older people. Not tonight. Tonight, I got to stay home and it would be nothing but TV watching and ice-cream sandwiches. Only one thing made me fright-fully cautious about the night. Guppy was my babysitter. Leaving Guppy in charge was like ringing the bell for a heavyweight fight. Instead of relaxing and enjoying myself, I might just end up in boot camp. I hoped she would start talking on the phone with her friends and leave me alone, for once. Our parents finally left and I headed to the den to turn on the tube. Everything was going well and I thought maybe I was worried for nothing. Then, the doorway darkened with the shadow of something dreadfully evil. My whole body grew numb, like a dead leaf.

Guppy stood there, with her hands on her hips, like a great sumo wrestler before a match. I tried to scream but nothing came out, just air. "Get up, you maggot boy!" she screamed. I sighed in agony as I got off the couch. BOOM! Her fist sank into my chest like a spoon sinking into pudding. The drill sergeant was in rare form. "Get upstairs and wash those dishes," she barked.

Pretty soon, not only was I washing the dishes but also cooking her dinner. I was waiting on her hand and foot. I was at her beck and call. This was the pits and I knew what I had to do. Escape. If only I could get past her room without being seen, I could sneak out to my friend Bigfella's house across the street until Mama came home. I would have to be as quiet as a cheetah.

I began my descent down our squeaky stairs, through

the living room, heading for the basement to the side door. I knew the front door made too much noise, but the side door was perfect. Thirteen steps and I was home-free. I finally got to the side door and ever so quietly began to open it. It was pitch black, so I had to feel my way to the door. Just a few steps to the freedom I desperately needed.

Then, in the dark, I felt myself being lifted off my feet by the collar of my shirt. Oh no, it was the sergeant. "Where do you think you're going, maggot?"
My heart sank into my underwear and then onto the floor in the form of a wet puddle. I knew I was in trouble. The night I imagined would be full of fun and relaxation became sheer terror—and it was just beginning.

A MOVIE OF SERIOUS TERROR BY T. BROWN
THE GUP
When a day at the movies goes wrong
IN ASSOCIATION WITH ARTISTRY DESIGN
A AD&I ENTERTAINMENT PRODUCTION STARRING GUPPY S.
EXECUTIVE PRODUCER T. BROWN
B RATED B FOR BULLIES
SUITABLE FOR ALL AGES

STORY ELEVEN

A Day At The Movies

It was the third Saturday of the month. The day Guppy's dad, Willie Lou, came to spend the day with her. I usually went along because Guppy hated her dad and she wouldn't talk to him. I was excited because Willie was great. He took us everywhere to enjoy everything, and since Guppy never talked it was like he and I were by ourselves. It was as if he was my dad instead of Guppy's.

Today was extra special because he was taking us to the movies. I loved going to the movies with Willie because we always went to the ghetto cinemas. It was great because the cinema was so different than the cinemas in the suburbs. The people reminded me of being around my own family members. It was like going to the movies with your aunts and uncles. The other great thing about it was the food. Soul food. It was like going to a family cookout at the movies, hot metts, barbeque chicken, and fries and burgers. Sometimes the owner would even sell sweet potato pie.

There were so many different characters at this cinema, it made watching a movie an interactive experience. Everyone talked to the screen as if it could answer back. There would be boos and howls for the bad guys and screams and claps for the good guys. People would stand up during scary parts and shout at the screen, "Get out of the way, girl! Can't you see he's behind the door?" Sometimes there were even fights, but most of the time it ended just fine. I remember when a woman once jumped up in her seat, screaming that there was a rat under her feet. Someone in the crowd yelled, "Sit down and shut up lady!" Everybody laughed, and she sat down and shut up. Things just had a way of working themselves out.

I always left the cinema feeling like I had gotten so much more than a movie and popcorn. I felt as if I had spent the day with my family, a theater full of cousins, aunts, and uncles. Guppy did as she always did when we left the cinema, walked with her arms folded, saying nothing. On the way home, I thought about how good of a time I had had that day. And I wondered if Guppy would remember times like this when we were older or if she was just letting this all pass her by while she was mad at the world.

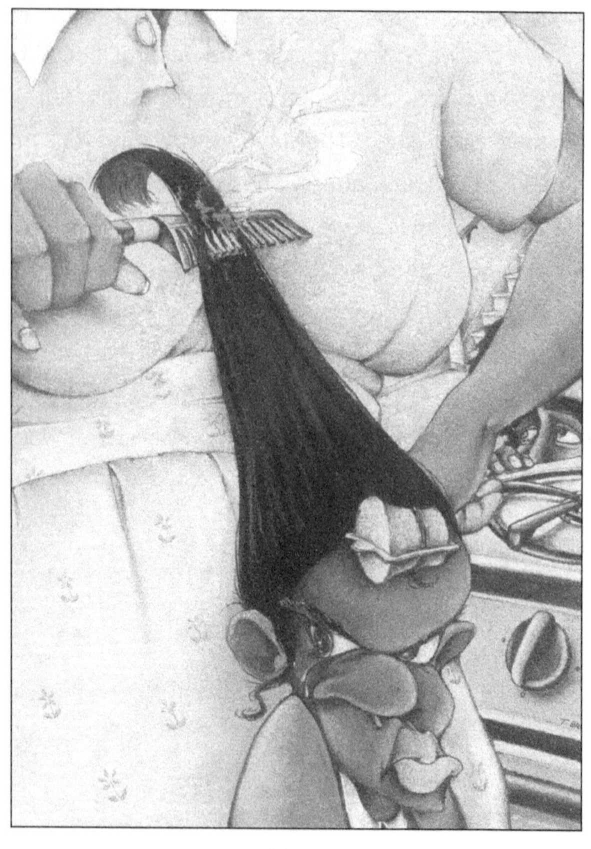

STORY TWELVE

SLOBBER AND TEARS

It was early Sunday morning. Gospel music was playing on the radio atop the refrigerator in the kitchen, and sunlight beamed through my bedroom window as the smell of homemade pancakes filled my room. I didn't mind being in church all day if the days started like this. I always rushed to get cleaned up so I could be the first to attack that stack of pancakes.

For Guppy, mornings were boot camp. She was usually grumpier than two cats trying to sleep in a chicken coop; and when she came to the table, she always looked like she had not washed her face and just rolled out of bed and showed up, the crust from sleep still in the corners of her mouth. Mama always made us say our blessings before we ate one bite, but the funny thing was, I never heard Guppy say her blessings. I wondered if she said anything at all. If she did say something, I'm sure it was mean.

Guppy lapped up her pancakes like a pack of wild hyenas, the syrup still caught in the corners of her mouth. After breakfast, Mama would have me clean the kitchen and then get dressed for church. She said the same dreaded six words every week. We prepared ourselves for it each Sunday, the drama, the agony, the thirty-minute ordeal of terror about to take place—all brought on by those six simple words: "Guppy, time to get your hair done."

This was one of the few times I ever saw Guppy completely powerless. She hated getting her hair done and she hated the dreadful iron-hot combs Mama used on her head. They must have weighed twenty-three pounds each. Those big, black, hot combs looked like the inside of a charcoal grill. The air in the kitchen was quickly filled with the stench of charred hair and burnt grease. Tension filled the room in anticipation of the first sizzle as the hot instrument of agony touched Guppy's greasy, tender scalp. We all cringed as Guppy's lungs filled with air to soon be released in the form of a chilling shriek.

This day, Guppy had met her match. One small instrument seemed to subdue her instantly, somehow doing what mere mortals could not: tame Guppy. Each time Mama reached for that hot comb, tears would stream down Guppy's face, symbolizing her defeat. Her face was tainted with trails of slobber and tears, but she knew if she protested the slightest bit, her fate would be sealed by a burn mark on her scalp. If things really got out of hand, Mama would snap her wrist quicker than a cat's blink, unleashing the full power of the hot comb. One pop on the head with that hot comb and Guppy was frozen in sheer agony. Those marks served as battle scars and reminders of the hell she went through on Sundays. They served as a reminder of who was really in control that day. For those thirty minutes, Guppy was a prisoner to the black woman's hair ritual. A tradition passed down from mother to daughter. I felt sorry for Guppy, trapped by the charred iron goddess. I was always the first one to see Guppy after Mama was finished with her hair, and I couldn't help but wonder how something so agonizing could tame such an ornery little girl. For a few moments, Guppy was changed. Transformed. For that brief moment, evil Guppy seemed to have disappeared in a shroud of beautiful black bangs and shiny curls.

For a moment, Guppy looked like a nice, little girl again. Just the way I remembered.

71

STORY TWELVE

I Don't Like Her Either

It was that time again. The day Guppy hated. The day her biological dad picked her up. I saw him just as much as Guppy because I always had to go along to make Guppy feel in control. Actually, our mom wanted me to go because, in a way, he was a father figure to me. I didn't mind going because it was like having a birthday every month.

Today, we were going to meet one of his girl-friends. I think Guppy was nervous because this could, after all, be her new stepmom. I wasn't worried about Guppy, I was worried for that lady. Boy, was she in for a surprise. There was only one Guppy and once you met her, you did not forget her. Mean like a pit full of snakes. Guppy could look at you and her eyes would go through you like a hot poker. This lady was in for a treat, a pure, potent dose of Guppy Lenore Shalinqua.

After Guppy's dad picked us up, he took us to his house to pick up his girlfriend. We were going to dinner. Guppy did not say a word, as usual. When we walked into his house, a small voice greeted us. "You must be Manny." Then, I saw her. She was more beautiful than I had imagined. She was like an enchanted black mermaid. She was like an ancient black princess that somehow got dropped off in our time. The room began to smile with her beauty … then Guppy came in the house. I didn't see what happened, but before the nice lady could even finish greeting Guppy, the room seemed to turn dark.
"You must be Guppy; such a pretty, little girl," she commented.

All of a sudden, Guppy let out a scream so loud I thought my clothes were going to peel off. "I hate you! I hate you, you black witch!" and she ran out of the house. From that point on, I knew Guppy would never like any woman her dad brought home. It didn't matter if she was the Queen of Sheba. It just wasn't going to work. I always knew in my heart that Guppy only wanted to see one woman with her dad and that woman was Mama.

We eventually went to dinner with the beautiful lady and, of course, Guppy didn't eat a bite, never said a word, continuing to protest the union. Her dad was so embarrassed and disappointed, I felt bad for him. Everyone was quiet during the ride home. As soon as we pulled into our driveway, Guppy bolted out of the car like a starved cheetah, never even saying goodbye. I was sure she was going to tell Mama all about the new lady.

I said goodbye and thanks as I always did. The nice lady kissed me on the cheek and told me I was a sweet boy. I'd never wash that cheek again. As they drove away, I couldn't help thinking about how upset Guppy was today. Then, for the first time, I thought about how it would be if Guppy's dad was my dad too. Maybe Guppy was on to something after all.

THE END

ACKNOWLEDGEMENTS

Troy Brown would like to thank his family for their patience and his many friends growing up within his modest Hollydale community. Thanks to my sons Quentin and Xavier for their daily inspiration and my excitable wife Sherie for her unwavering committment to our dreams together.

The text for this book is set in Verdana Regular.
The Display type is Trajon Pro and Palatino.
The Title Logo/Identity was designed by David Vermett.
The illustrations are rendered in graphite, watercolor and pastel.

Editor: Mary Jo Zazueta, To The Point Solutions

About the Author...

Troy Brown grew up in the midwest in a small African American Community called Hollydale located in a Suburb of Cincinnati, Ohio. He learned important life lessons from neighbors and friends that cared deeply about the community. Hollydale became an inspiration and true definition of what community was about to Troy. Brown has a distinguished career as a Graphic Designer, Art Director, Illustrator and currently is a professor of art. He, his wife and two sons reside in North Carolina where he writes and illustrates books between enjoying time at the beach. His other titles are *Lois and the Red Balloon, Feathers* and *Xavier's Book of Sometimes.*

Visit Troy's website to see what else he's up to these days at www.brownsugarpress.com.

The Sketchbook Legends was born out of events of little Manny McCloud's childhood. This collection of short stories chronicles not only the perils of living with bullies in everyday life, but manages to expose a glimmer of light in the darkest human moments.